MW01179154

Dating and Relationships

Relationships

Navigating the Social Scene

A YOUNG MAN'S GUIDE
TO CONTEMPORARY ISSUES™

Dating and Relationships
Navigating the Social Scene

Arie Kaplan

ROSEN
PUBLISHING®

New York

Published in 2012 by The Rosen Publishing Group, Inc.
29 East 21st Street, New York, NY 10010

Library of Congress Cataloging-in-Publication Data

Kaplan, Arie.
Dating and relationships: navigating the social scene/Arie Kaplan.
    p. cm.—(A young man's guide to contemporary issues)
Includes bibliographical references and index.
ISBN 978-1-4488-5523-0 (library binding)
1. Interpersonal relations—Juvenile literature.
2. Teenage boys—Juvenile literature.
3. Dating (Social customs)—Juvenile literature. I. Title.
HM1106.K365 2012
155.5'18—dc22

                                                    2011013322

Manufactured in the United States of America

CPSIA Compliance Information: Batch #W12YA: For further information, contact Rosen Publishing, New York, New York, at 1-800-237-9932.

Contents

INTRODUCTION

There are many reasons why you might be reading this book. Perhaps you've got a friend who hasn't been acting very friendly lately. Maybe you're having trouble relating to your parents. Or maybe you're entering into your first real romantic relationship, and you've found that the prospect of real intimacy frightens you.

Part of being a teenager is having your first real "adult" relationships with other people—be they your

friends, parents, siblings, or a boyfriend or girl-friend. Suddenly, the stakes are higher, your emotions are stronger, relationship dynamics are shifting, and everything feels more ... real. Discovering a way to navigate through the tough terrain of peer, sibling, and parental relationships as an adolescent male is difficult. And with recent changes in technology, the rules of personal conduct and communication have also changed. It's not easy. That's where this book comes in.

This book explores the home, family, and relationship issues that boys may encounter during the teen years. Learning to grapple with the adolescent dating scene, with the perils and pitfalls of friendships, and with your own shifting role in your family is something that isn't done all at once. You may wonder why it is that your parents never seem to really "get" you. You may be concerned that your girlfriend or boyfriend is pressuring you to have sex and that you're not ready. You might think that your best friend said or did something cruel or manipulative. You might be saddened or confused by a long-term friendship that begins to change or even ends. You might even have a crush on someone, but you're unsure about how to approach him or her.

It may be comforting to know that you aren't alone in your worries. There are millions of young men all around the world who are struggling with the same issues as you are.

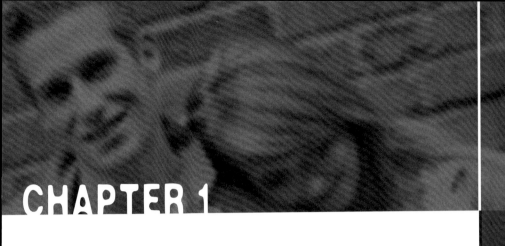

CHAPTER 1

CULTURAL STEREOTYPES

Are you familiar with the nursery rhyme "What are little boys made of? Snips and snails and puppy dogs' tails"? According to that same rhyme, little girls are made of "Sugar and spice, and everything nice." Many believe these firmly held stereotypes about boys and girls: boys are supposed to be scrappy, dirty, and violent, and girls are proper and delicate, possessing a sweet disposition. Lately, these old models have been demolished to make way for new ones. However, many people cling to the old models, frightened to admit that the new models even exist. But they do. And that's a good thing, especially if you're a teenage boy!

For one thing, you now have many more emotional and behavioral options than you used to. Typically, teenage boys often have difficulty confronting their emotions. The typical "masculine" responses to stress are anger and emotional withdrawal. Some boys cannot express their feelings in words. They're not socialized to do so, as girls

are. According to the book *Raising Cain: Protecting the Emotional Life of Boys,* by Dan Kindlon and Michael Thompson, many boys lack the necessary "emotional vocabulary"—the correct way of expressing their emotions verbally via any way other than anger or aggression. However, the old model is changing in some ways. In fact,

Many adolescent boys worry about their appearance, including such issues as skin, posture, hair, and fashion.

today the average teenage boy usually has the same self-esteem issues as his female counterpart.

Boys' self-esteem issues often include height, weight, appearance (skin, posture, hair, fashion), and athletic prowess. Recent studies show that boys are just as concerned with their bodies and their appearance as girls are.

Males often fall in love just as hard as girls during adolescence. Like their female counterparts, young males desire meaningful relationships, and they are looking for romance—not merely sex—within those relationships. Many boys today say that girls are the ones in the relationship who hold most of the power. Some studies even suggest that young men are more interested in romance and emotional connection than their female partners. There are more emotionally responsive young males out there than we might think.

Who Is "Different"?

If you're an adolescent male, the likelihood is that the other kids at school aren't very tolerant of people who are "different." They're "weird," they're "bizarre," and worst of all, they're exposed to ridicule. Teenagers use insults, slurs, and other verbal slings and arrows to psychologically taunt those who are different. But what does it mean to be different?

There are many ways to become the proverbial odd man out. Perhaps you're the only member of a certain ethnic or religious group in your class. Unfortunately, while most teens know not to sink so low as to resort to ethnic or racial slurs, a small but vocal number of teens might find making fun of someone's background to be the height of hilarity. These kind of slurs and taunts can also be a desperate and dirty shortcut to social status—one can raise one's standing on the social ladder by tearing someone else down.

A NEW MANHOOD

A paradigm shift has occurred regarding the way popular culture views adolescent males. Whereas, in the 1970s and 1980s, and even into the late 1990s, it was common for movie audiences to see raunchy, obnoxious characters like Bluto (played by John Belushi) in *Animal House* or Stifler (played by Seann William Scott) in *American Pie*, the Hollywood stereotype of the American teen male is changing as well. We still see Bluto-like characters, like Seth (Jonah Hill) in 2007's *Superbad*. Yet Seth was balanced in that movie by the more sensitive, thoughtful, and reserved Evan (Michael Cera). By the end of the movie, Seth himself was revealed to have a sensitive, vulnerable side, one that was completely lacking in Bluto or Stifler.

In fact, in films like *Superbad*, the more obnoxious characters use their raunchy humor as a defense mechanism. Beneath it all, they're deeply insecure. The Michael Cera model of the sensitive, vulnerable teen male has increasingly been seen in films of the last decade, from *Spider-Man*'s Tobey Maguire (2002) to virtually any film starring Jessie Eisenberg—*The Squid and the Whale* (2005), *Adventureland* (2009), *Zombieland* (2009), *Solitary Man* (2009), and even *The Social Network* (2010), in which he plays Mark Zuckerberg, the creator of Facebook.

This also applies to homophobia. If you're a gay teen, you might be the only out gay kid in your school, or maybe you're still in the closet. Unfortunately, in this day and age, it's common for teens to use the word "gay" as a synonym for "weak" or "lame." They often don't even realize how hurtful their words might be to someone who actually is gay. These slurs are also wildly inaccurate, for

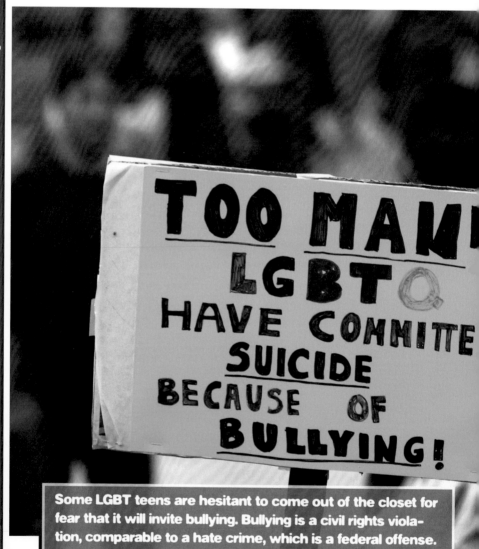

Some LGBT teens are hesitant to come out of the closet for fear that it will invite bullying. Bullying is a civil rights violation, comparable to a hate crime, which is a federal offense.

there is absolutely nothing weak about gay people. The struggles they face often make them, in fact, stronger and tougher than those people who do not face such daily adversity and lack of acceptance.

In many cases, your peers at school may simply need to be educated about the words they use. For example, just as "gay" can mean "weak" in adolescent slang, there

are slurs regarding someone's intelligence that refer to people with developmental disabilities. To someone who is developmentally disabled—or who has a friend or relative who is—these casually tossed and taunting words can be toxic. Similarly, the smartest kids in class will often be singled out for taunts, due to their "geeky" qualities. So, what do we learn from this?

For one thing, if everybody has something about them that singles them out for potential insults, due to their race, religion, sexual orientation, or level of academic achievement, then what is normal? Who is normal? The answer: no one. And everyone. Because if no one is normal, everyone is. How do you combat the prejudice, the igno-rance, the cruel jokes made at the expense of those who don't realize this?

The first step is to tell the people making those jokes that their words hurt you or people you care about, and that you would appreciate it if they didn't use that sort of language. If you've heard anyone making threat-ening remarks toward people of a different race, religion, or sexual orientation—or if they've made those remarks to you—you should immediately contact an authority figure and tell him/her what you've heard. If you fear that you'll become the victim of the people who made those threats if you report the incident, you should ask to remain anonymous.

Also, it's a good idea to start a dialogue in your school about diversity of all kinds. Perhaps one of your teachers can help you get the discussion going. The goal here is to get students of various backgrounds to talk about their feelings and experiences and to begin an open dialogue. That way, no one will feel left out. Hopefully, everyone will come to realize that in some way each of us is "different," that difference is enriching, and it makes the world a far more interesting and stimulating place.

Big Bully

When you're a young child, the bully is the kid on the playground who punches the smaller, weaker children, steals their lunch money, or terrorizes them with pranks and mischief. A good example of this is the character Nelson Muntz from the TV show *The Simpsons*. However, as one

If you're being bullied, you should tell an adult whom you trust. As of this writing, forty-five states have enacted antibullying laws.

gets older and enters junior high and high school, bullies tend to focus less on doling out physical harassment and more on inflicting emotional or social harm. They do this largely by targeting their victims' worst anxieties. Especially among boys, bullies can zoom in on their targets' nervousness about sex, sexual orientation, self-image, and perceived physical shortcomings. Adolescent boys—already prone to fears and insecurities about sex, masculinity, body image, and the like—are easy prey for these bullies.

Bullies often target victims because of their physical appearance—they may be skinny and weak or overweight, for example. Yet bullies also often focus on a victim's race, religion, gender, disability, or sexual orientation. For this reason, bullying is a civil rights violation comparable to harassment or even a hate crime (which is a federal offense). As of this writing, forty-five states have adopted antibullying laws. If you're being bullied, you should tell an adult whom you trust, whether it's a teacher, coach, school administrator, or your parents, so that they can handle it in a professional manner.

Technology has changed the very nature of human relationships. This is true of bullying as well, and nowhere is this clearer than in the realm of cyberspace. A detailed discussion of cyberbullying can be found in chapter 7, "Your Online Profile."

CHAPTER 2

FRIENDSHIPS AND "ENEMYSHIPS"

The young male in today's society occupies an interesting space, emotionally speaking. On one hand, he is bound to old notions of machismo (acting "macho") and other timeworn clichés of masculine behavior. On the other hand, as words like "metrosexual" (a heterosexual male who takes great pride and care in his appearance, through clothes, grooming, etc.), "bromance" (a platonic friendship between men that is as emotionally rich and satisfying as their romantic relationships), and other catch-phrases from throughout the last decade indicate, he is also at the forefront of a new and shifting era in male attitudes. Before we discuss what new trends are developing in male friendships, it's a good idea to go over exactly what makes male friendships specifically "male."

Bonding and Boasting

Boys have certain ways of bonding with each other, just as girls do. Sometimes it involves sports, cars, the great

Some adolescent boys put on a tough facade to mask their own insecurities.

outdoors, or harmless horseplay. Other forms of male bonding, however, aren't always so benign. Male bonding can often include taunting about physical shortcomings, as well as bragging about one's own romantic conquests. This is often a defense mechanism, and some teenage boys are prone to talk about women in a very cruel, crass way, especially about sexual activity.

When teenage boys talk like this, you can bet that they have very little real-world experience with sexual intercourse. This is given away by the fact that their boastfulness takes on a sort of exaggerated quality. This is partially because boys with very little experience in romantic relationships tend to see girls as foreign and even frightening. They both want and are scared off by the prospect of real intimacy. However, they want to boost their "masculine" image among their friends, so they boast. Other young men respond to and mimic this sort of boastfulness because they want to be "one of the boys." They don't want to stay silent or object and risk being identified and taunted as someone who is somehow less than masculine. Boys' boasting is less about sex, or relationships with women, than it is about male camaraderie. Nobody wants to feel like they're going through something all alone, and nobody wants to be singled out for scorn by not participating in the often vulgar and derogatory discussion.

"Come On, Everyone's Doing It ..."

This leads us into another area: peer pressure. If you're a teenage boy, perhaps you've felt pressure to be sexually active or at least to put up a front implying that you've got quite a bit of "experi-ence" in this area. Don't buy into the hype. Any kind of peer pressure comes from insecurity on the part of the person who is pressuring you. He or she is the one with the problem, not you.

Peer pressure can present itself in different ways. Obviously, when your friends try to tempt you into drinking alco-holic beverages or using drugs, that's peer pres-sure. However, when one of your friends tries to rope you into helping him humiliate or bully someone, that, too, is peer pressure. The bot-tom line is, you don't have to do anything that you don't want to do,

especially if it's something that gives you a bad feeling inside. That's called a "gut instinct," and if your gut instinct tells you that whatever your friend is telling you to do is something you'll later regret, then you should

When your friends try to rope you into drinking alcoholic beverages or using drugs, that's peer pressure.

decline. Your friend may tease you for not choosing to join in his "fun," but in the end, you'll avoid trouble, you won't harm anyone, you'll retain your self-respect, and you'll feel good about that.

Ten Great Questions

TO ASK YOUR GUIDANCE COUNSELOR

1.
How can I stop fighting with my parents and siblings?

2.
Why is one of my oldest friendships dying?

3.
How can I be sure my new friend is really a friend?

4.
What should I do if my friends don't like my reluctance to do the things they're trying to make me do?

5.
Why do people drink, smoke, or use drugs?

6.
How can I help a friend who is abusing drugs or alcohol?

7.
How can I tell if the person I like likes me back?

8.
When do you know that you're ready for sex?

9.
How do I maintain my old friendships now that I have a girl/boyfriend?

10.
How do I get over a breakup with my girl/boyfriend?

When Friends Become "Frenemies"

It's traditionally believed that when teenage boys are mean to one another, it's in a straightforward, physical, "honest" way—grabbing each other in a headlock, punching each other in the stomach. Meanwhile, teenage girls are thought to be just as cruel, but in a more calculating, sneaky, and deceitful way. Girls are thought to wreak more psychological damage on their victims, while boys just pummel theirs. But what's changing is that boys are beginning to use these more psychologically aggressive tactics as well.

When you know someone—a boy or a girl—who says you're a friend but doesn't act like it, chances are he or she isn't really your friend. The term "frenemy" is used to describe a combative, love-hate, friend-enemy relationship. Put simply, a frenemy is an enemy disguised as a friend. How do you know if your friend is really a frenemy? Friends who don't respect certain basic ground rules of social conduct—or friends who don't consistently show you common courtesy or respect—may be considered frenemies.

For example, friends who don't return your phone calls or texts may be frenemies. So, too, are "friends" who are nice to your face but talk trash about you behind your back to your other friends—or worse, to your enemies. Friends who date your ex-girlfriends or ex-boyfriends are frenemies. This doesn't always mean that your frenemy is consciously acting in a malicious or vindictive way toward you. He

Friends who don't return your phone calls or texts, or who otherwise leave you hanging, might be considered frenemies.

might not even be aware that he's acting this way. It could simply be a symptom that you and he are drifting apart as friends. This is always sad when it happens, but sometimes old friendships wilt, and just as often, new ones are bound to flourish.

When Frenemies Become All-Out Enemies

Sometimes frenemies become full-fledged enemies. There are often warning signs that will tell you this is happening. People who want you to do things to maintain a certain "cool" image—like drinking or smoking or bullying some-one lower on the ladder of social status—do not value you for who you really are. These are opportunistic, fly-by-night friends on whom you can't rely. Friends who are unsupport-ive, especially in your times of need, are also not your friends. A true friend will "have your back" all the time, not just when it's convenient to do so.

Similarly, if you have a friend who indulges in drugs or alcohol, this person might develop addictions that he can't control. When people are addicted to controlled sub-stances, they often become slaves to it. Their personalities change, and they will say and do things that no real friend would. A drug addict or alcoholic who is taking no steps toward sobriety or rehabilitation is no longer your friend. That's because he's no longer the same person he was when he was sober. His primary and most important rela-tionship is with his drug. He has no room for friends and

If your friend is a drug addict or alcoholic who is taking no steps toward rehabilitation, that person can no longer act as a true friend to you.

DEALING WITH YOUR FRENEMY

If you think that you're stuck in a frenemy situation, there are a few things that you can do. For one thing, if your friend's less admirable, more mean-spirited qualities surface only when he's angry or tense, avoid him during those times. Remember that it's your friend's problem to solve, and you can only help when you are being treated in a decent and respectful manner. You don't need to become infected with your friend's negative energy. Don't convince yourself that this situation is all your fault. Some of us have a tendency to blame ourselves or internalize things. Don't fall into this trap. Instead, hang out with your other, more positive friends. These are friends who don't feel like "enemies in friend's clothing" and who consistently make you feel liked, appreciated, and valued.

very little leftover emotional energy to offer. Addicts are also often intensely selfish, obsessed only with obtaining their next fix. They will use you, if necessary, to obtain that goal, but they will offer you nothing in the way of true friendship.

As a friend, you can certainly try to help him get the treatment and counseling he needs. If you have to lose your friend because that person's life is tangled in a web of drugs or alcohol, it's better to lose that friend than to have him pull you down with him.

CHAPTER 3

FAMILY RELATIONSHIPS

It wasn't so long ago that most Americans thought they knew what a household was: a husband, a wife, and two or three children. In recent years, however, we've come to understand that this isn't the only valid version of the family unit. With divorce rates skyrocketing over the past few decades, and with gay and lesbian couples becoming more and more prominent and broadly accepted, there are many other alternative models to consider when talking about the family unit. Some other family structures that have become more common in recent years include step-parenting, coparenting grandparents raising grandchildren, and single parents. But, no matter the family structure, most children have a father and a mother, or role models who fulfill those functions.

The Legacy of the Father

Among boys who have fathers (or father figures), the most emotionally attuned and well-adjusted sons are usually the ones who have had caring, comforting relationships with their dads. However, achieving this kind of warm and nurturing relationship with a male parent is not always easy. One of the reasons for this is that many fathers unconsciously mimic the emotionally distant nature of the male role models they've known throughout their lives.

Problems tend to arise when sons reach adolescence. Even a father who has had a fairly solid relationship with his son suddenly finds himself with a sullen teen who challenges his parental authority at every turn. Such fathers, taken unawares by their son's behavior, often fall back on what they were taught by their own fathers—to become distant, angry, or authoritarian. This becomes a vicious cycle. How can this cycle be avoided?

Boys model their father's behavior all throughout their childhood. This is how boys learn to become men, but it also means that fathers must be very conscious about how they act and react and what they say. When a father and son are shooting hoops or playing a videogame, and the father loses, does the father yell and get angry, or does he laugh it off and take it in stride? Does he admit when he's wrong, or does he deny that he's ever wrong? How a father responds to his own shortcomings, limitations, and mistakes teaches his son an invaluable lesson about emotional honesty and coping skills.

What does this mean for fathers and their adolescent sons? As a teenager, you still need your father emotionally, but you might not be willing to admit this. This is because a teenager's continued emotional dependence on his father is an uncomfortable reminder that he is still, in some ways,

a child. On the other hand, many fathers of teenage boys still like to maintain a tight grip on their interactions with their sons—being in control of the conversations, feeling that they're always "in the know." They may not realize that their sons are chafing under their control.

When fathers listen to their children, rather than trying to control the conversation, the relationships become much more solid and mutually sustaining.

So, what can be done? Fathers need to listen to their children, to validate their opinions and not try to control the situation. If you came home and told your dad that you wanted to be an actor, he could have two reactions: He could explode and lecture you on how you were throwing your life away, or he could patiently listen and take a genuine interest in this new passion of yours. Even if, deep down, your father thought that this was a poor decision on your part, at least he would be hearing you out, respecting your opinion, encouraging and supporting your enthusiasm, and ceding control of the situation. You'd be on equal ground, and that's where everyone wants to be.

Momma's Boy?

What about the relationship between adolescent males and their mothers? Traditionally, the mother is a young boy's emotional lifeline. She offers him a shoulder to cry on. She might, in fact, be the only person in whose presence a boy feels comfortable crying or expressing emotional vulnerability. However, during adolescence, a mother might not realize that her son's attitudes and needs are changing, and conflict will result.

This often happens because teenage boys are making the move toward independence, and many mothers see this straining toward independence as a rejection of their love. Of course, it isn't rejection, and what all mothers of teenage boys need to understand is that their influence, which was all-important in their son's early years, has now been at least partly eclipsed by the influence of their son's peer group. In short, where you once sought approval and advice solely from your parents, you now also receive much of that approval and advice from your friends. However, this doesn't mean that your mother—and her counsel—is no longer important to your life. It's simply that your mother's opinion is now one of several that you solicit.

Mothers can often serve as an emotional lifeline for a young boy.

There are also some families in which a boy values his mother's opinion too much. He may be frightened of provoking his mother's disapproval and would do—or not do—anything to avoid that. Some boys seek their mother's approval so often that they don't feel confident in making their own decisions. This situation is sometimes the result of mothers who are too involved in their adolescent sons' lives and insist on micromanaging them.

It's important to understand that this isn't done with any malicious intent on the part of the mother; quite the opposite, in fact. She's only trying to help her son, and, when her son was younger and more helpless, the fact that she made decisions for him was no doubt helpful. However, when boys reach their teen years, they need to understand that it's OK to fail, that life is not perfect, and that there will not always be a maternal safety net waiting below them at all times. They must also accept that they will not always please their mother or avoid her disapproval. They must begin learning how to live their lives independently and make smart decisions that are best for them. Mothers usually understand this, and most of them give their sons enough breathing room. When they don't, it leads their sons toward confusion and indecisiveness.

The teen years are when many boys distance themselves emotionally from their mothers. They don't want to be labeled a "momma's boy" and often don't want to risk being seen in public hugging or kissing their mother. During adolescence, when the approval of one's friends is paramount, this attitude is understandable. However, it is possible to walk a middle ground between being a so-called momma's boy and being emotionally detached from one's mother. Even during adolescence, there's no shame in having a private chat with your mother to talk about your problems, worries, and fears. Boys, whether they realize it or not, rely on their mother's warmth and encouragement of emotional openness. A close, healthy, respectful, and affectionate relationship with his mother prepares a boy for the emotional openness he'll need to create and benefit from in later adult relationships, including romantic ones.

Two Moms or Two Dads: Same-Sex Parents

Family models other than father-mother-children exist and are becoming increasingly common and widely accepted. Children benefit from both male and female role models. Does this mean that children of same-sex parents are any worse off? No, they are not. Children who have gay or lesbian parents experience as much joy, happiness, nurturing, frustration, anger, sadness, and rich and complex family dynamics as children of heterosexual couples. In the end, families are just families. Family dynamics are universal, regardless of the gender or sexual orientation of the parents. One's sexual orientation has nothing to do with one's ability to parent a child or the development of one's parenting skills. The ability to give and receive love is what is primarily required, and everyone has that potential.

American society is, slowly but surely, coming to accept this fact. This is reflected in the media as well. Not long ago, gay and lesbian couples were rarely seen in movies and television shows. Now, we've reached a point where there are Oscar-nominated films like *The Kids Are All Right* (2010), which centers around a lesbian couple (played by Annette Bening and Julianne Moore), who are parents to two teenagers.

Films like *The Kids Are All Right* point out that gay and lesbian parents create healthy, nurturing, and supportive

Films like *The Kids Are All Right* show that gay and lesbian parents create healthy, nurturing, and supportive families, just like those headed by a heterosexual couple.

families just like those headed by a mother and a father. However, not everyone realizes this. If you've ever been taunted for being the child of gay or lesbian parents, you should realize that the person who's making fun of you is simply revealing his or her own insecurity. Homophobia, like all other kinds of prejudice, is born of ignorance and fear. It has everything to do with the homophobic person and his or her problems and nothing to do with you or your family. Try to remain confident and secure in the love your family gives you, and don't let anyone make you doubt your family's worth.

CHAPTER 4

School Ties

School is hard for just about every teenager, from the loneliest outsiders to the most popular homecoming king and queen. Adult men and women often remember high school as the time when they received their most punishing psychological wounds, often delivered by taunts, put-downs, social ostracism (shunning), and physical bullying. Boys are expected to endure this abuse without shedding a tear.

Bottled-Up Anger

Traditionally, boys are encouraged to adopt "tough" behavior and to have a rough-and-tumble attitude. They're expected to fight back and give as good as they get. Fight fire with fire. However, some boys fashion a psychological shell of "toughness" that becomes difficult to remove after it is no longer needed. This defensive shell can prevent them from forming meaningful relationships with others, including their friends at school. These boys have been taught that it's best to swallow one's feelings. By internalizing, or bottling up, their feelings, they become a walking powder keg, and their anger can explode at any time. Even more tragic is the fact that this anger is often directed at people who aren't the true source of their frustration.

The way to keep this from happening is for young men to externalize what they've been taught to internalize. But how? For one thing, where does this internalized anger come from? In teenage boys, it usually comes from insecurity, which in turn comes from being on the bottom of the social food chain at school (or fearing the possibility of slipping to the bottom). Think about it: the angry, frustrated bullies you've known at school usually aren't the class president or the quarterback of the football team, but rather the kid who's known as an outsider or social pariah. Or sometimes the bully exists on the fringes of the cool crowd and wants to solidify his shaky position by pushing someone weaker down. His role can even be to entertain the cool kids above him by harassing and humiliating those below him. But everyone—popular or unpopular or somewhere in between—can feel socially insecure and vulnerable. This can create anxiety and anger, and it can be directed at innocent victims. What do you do if you've held on to these negative feelings and bottled them up inside of you?

The first step is to identify and articulate what you're really angry about. What's really bugging you? If boys in our society aren't taught to talk about their feelings (and for the most part, they're not), this may be an alien concept to many of them. If you can articulate exactly why you're angry,

and with whom you're angry, you'll be able to deal with your anger in a healthy, productive way, rather than simply taking out your emotions on the nearest helpless target.

Also, learning to talk through your problems—rather than quickly acting on your anger—can be a great way to defuse a potentially violent situation, a situation you may come to regret. You'd be surprised how relieved

Young men who learn communication skills early in life will be more likely to talk out their disagreements, rather than letting them escalate into physical confrontations.

you'll feel once you simply talk about what's on your mind. Having a good talk with your friends at school can make you feel a hundred percent better. If you're talking to the person with whom you are angry, the two of you might be able to make peace and avoid a conflict that can rapidly spin out of control and have long-lasting social consequences.

Cliques

Jocks. Stoners. Nerds. Goths. Preppies. Cliques are as much a part of the teenage experience as prom dates and awkwardness. But what constitutes a clique? A clique is a group of friends that hangs out together exclusively. Not sometimes, but every day. And it's a closed society; it is very difficult to break into—and even out of—a clique. As author Aisha Muharrar points out in her book *More Than a Label: Why What You Wear or Who You're With Doesn't Define Who You Are*, in cliques, there are usually either spoken or unspoken rules about letting in outsiders. This is what separates a clique from a friendship, which is nowhere near as exclusive.

Are you part of a clique? You might be part of one, even though you're not aware of it. Basically, you're part of a clique if you fit each of the following criteria:

- Do you and your friends wear the same types of clothing or do you talk in the same manner (using a specific type of slang or jargon identified with a particular group)?
- Is there a "leader" in your group of friends, i.e., someone in charge?
- Do you restrict people who are different from being in your group of friends?
- Do you feel like you and your friends are better than everyone else?

THE STRENGTH OF VULNERABILITY

Teenage boys are often expected to be rough, tough, wise-cracking, and emotionally blunted. The emotions they are "allowed" to express are usually frustration and anger. The age when it was somewhat acceptable to cry when hurt or sad passed sometime in middle school, according to society's prevailing norms. Yet you should know that being emotionally "vulnerable" doesn't mean being "weak." Simply because you felt something so deeply that it moved you to tears doesn't make you weak. You can take pride in the fact that you're an emotionally well-adjusted teenager who's on his way to becoming an emotionally well-adjusted adult. Meanwhile, those who would mock someone for showing emotional vulnerability are likely to experience frequent conflict, communication problems, and misunderstandings in their own lives. This often leads to a series of failed relationships with family, friends, and loved ones. In short, if the concept of a vulnerable male makes someone chuckle, or feel angry, frightened, or threatened, that's their problem, not yours.

This is not to say that friendships equal cliques. Most friends have some things in common; that's part of why they became friends in the first place. Maybe what brought you and your friends together was a shared love of football, or old movies, or videogames, or hip-hop. However, what separates friendships from cliques is the sense of exclusivity, and superiority, that often comes with cliques.

There's nothing innately negative about the concept of a clique. Unfortunately, however, members of cliques often ostracize students who are not like them and mock or ridicule those who don't "belong" within their group. Also, the idea that a clique has an official or unofficial "leader"—someone who makes the rules and directs the actions, attitudes, and

Unfortunately, members of cliques often ostracize those who are different from them and mock or ridicule those who don't "belong" within their group.

even thoughts of the members—can only eat away at the self-confidence and sense of independence and individuality of the other group members. This only adds to the already hefty laundry list of stressors that teenagers encounter on a daily basis. For this reason, the negatives of being in a clique far outweigh the positives.

Making new friends is part of what being a teenager is all about.

This doesn't mean that you should think twice before making new friends. Making new friends is part of what being a teenager is all about. However, teenagers should beware of letting themselves fall in with a clique. Instead, they should form emotionally healthy friendships. These should be the sort of friendships where, if they make new friends, their established friends won't feel threatened by the presence of an "outsider." When everyone in a group of friends is equally open to the concept of meeting new people and enjoying the variety of rich experiences life has to offer, only then can real emotional maturity and growth occur.

CHAPTER 5

COMMUNICATION

As a young man beginning to make your way in the world, you'll find that communication is the key to every sort of relationship. Whether you're dealing with your parents, friends, fellow students, girlfriend/boyfriend, teachers, or coworkers, you need to understand what the other party wants and needs—and be able to express your own wants and needs—if the relationship is going to work. Maintaining an ongoing dialogue with the people in your life cuts down on misunderstanding, hurt feelings, and missed opportunities. Also, it maximizes your potential for succeeding and reaching your goals in life.

Talking to Your Parents

It's often a good idea to come to your parents for advice, encouragement, and comfort. You might have bristled upon reading the preceding sentence, and if you did, that's not surprising. Many teenagers would rather confide in almost anyone else other than their parents.

This is because parents occasionally have a tendency to overreact, lecture, or talk down to their children, rather than engaging in a meaningful, two-way discussion with them. When a child reaches a certain age, he begins to strive for independence. If the child's parents are still talking to a fourteen-year-old the way they did when the child was eight, that creates frustration and resentment. This is a shame because parents really do have an enormous amount of wisdom to impart to their children. They've literally "been there, done that." So what can be done to ensure better communication between parents and children?

Parents need to listen, not lecture. They need to establish a "noninterference" policy (even if unspoken), and they need to hear you out. There's nothing teens hate more than when their parent doesn't listen, is patronizing, or lectures them about what they "need" to do. Sometimes, a teenager simply wants a sympathetic ear rather than advice or directives.

As a teenager, you can also try to communicate better with your parents. For example, you probably feel conflicted about venting—unloading all of your problems in one big cathartic rant—when you're with your friends. Maybe you feel that it would burden them, bore them, or make them think less of you. Whether that's true or not depends on the friend in question. Not so with parents.

You may be surprised to hear this, but venting is not only something they would usually welcome, it's something they'd most likely encourage. This is because, at this point in your life, your parents know that you have a great need for independence. They're both excited and terrified that you're growing into a new and different person. This

By confiding in your parents, you're unburdening yourself of your anxieties, while also keeping your relationship with your parents healthy and close.

terrifies them because they know that, inevitably, you'll be keeping secrets from them or that there are a great many things you'll only feel comfortable telling your friends. By actually confiding in them and telling them what's on your mind, you're unburdening yourself of your fears and anxieties. At the same time, you're keeping your relationship with your parents close and healthy.

Let's Talk About It

Perhaps you're dating someone who's not much of a talker and doesn't like to open up or share. If you're the exact opposite—that is, someone who prefers to talk through his emotions—this can be a tough relationship to navigate. In truth, the relationship will progress along a

Getting your significant other to talk to you more can be as simple as asking questions about how her day went.

much smoother path if you get your girlfriend or boyfriend to talk to you more. Then the lines of communication will be that much stronger, and your relationship will have an exponentially higher chance for success. But how do you get your significant other to talk to you more?

You can start by asking questions. Express a curiosity about how your girlfriend or boyfriend's day went, or how her or his article for the school paper is coming along. If your questions are usually met with curt, short answers, then perhaps it's time to probe deeper. Ask for details, but not in a way that would make your significant other uncomfortable. Instead, ask in a way that shows you care and shows you're truly interested. When you show an interest in your girlfriend or boyfriend's life, he or she will show an interest in yours, and the relationship will become enriched.

Sometimes listening is all you have to do to get someone to open up. People often just need someone to share their thoughts, feelings, joys, sorrows, fears, and hopes with. This is especially the case in the high school years, given all the drama that can occur in a single day.

Feelings?

As a teenage boy, all of this talk about feelings may make you nervous. You may not want to talk about your feelings. On the other hand, perhaps you are a boy who's very comfortable talking about his feelings, but you have other male friends who are more emotionally closed off, and this frustrates you. Some boys see emotional connectedness as a lack of strength, or more important, as a sign of weakness. However, nothing could be farther from the truth. You're at a crucial stage in your life, and this is a perfect time to practice a greater emotional connection to those around you.

A good place to start would be to name your feelings. Some boys are so conditioned to ignore their emotions that they don't even know there are names for what they're feeling. This isn't because they're ignorant; it's just that they haven't taken the time to examine and identify their feelings. In order to avoid allowing unexamined emotions to spill over unexpectedly and lead to arguments or misunderstandings, always remember to think before you speak. If you're angry, what are you really feeling, and with whom are you really upset? Once you figure that out and act accordingly, you'll find that the time you took to examine, understand, and name your emotions has allowed your temper to cool. This will prevent any rash displays of anger and instead encourage positive and healthy interactions that can help resolve the causes of your frustration.

Is That Really Constructive?

No matter what sort of relationship you're in, there's a difference between constructive criticism and nonconstructive criticism. Let's say that someone said or did something that offended you. Whether you're that person's sibling, son, or significant other, there is a delicate way to critique them. It's a way that will cut down on potential hurt feelings.

If you're talking to your significant other, be mindful of your tone of voice. If you say, "I'm upset," but you do it in a shrill, nervous manner, it will come off instantly as accusatory and aggressive. However, if you say it in a calm, relaxed manner, the person you're speaking to will be much more responsive. Also, explain how the other person's actions make you feel. For example, if you say, "I feel like you don't care about our relationship," instead of just jumping to the accusatory, "You don't care about our relationship," the discussion will be probably be much less combative.

The Direct Approach

We've spent some time talking about how you communicate with your significant other. But how do you take that first step to become someone's significant other? How do you ask someone out for the first time, and what if you've never done it before? Asking someone out can be a frightening experience. You risk rejection and hurt feelings. Because of this, it's a good idea to establish

some ground rules in order to lower the risk of rejection and maximize your own feelings of comfort and self-confidence.

If you're new to the dating scene, it's probably a good idea not to ask out a complete stranger. Instead, ask out

If you ask someone out and she declines, do not push it and try to pressure her to accept. No does mean no.

someone you already know or whom your friends know and like. You might even ask someone out who you think might already like you. This cuts down on the tension and makes it more likely that you'll have something in common with this person.

♂ JUST FRIENDS

What if you ask someone out, and she tells you that she "only likes you as a friend"? There's not really anything you can do in that situation. It's possible that this person will change her mind. However, you shouldn't spend any time hanging around and waiting or planning for that to happen.

Nobody likes to be rejected, but it happens to everyone. So, if you find yourself dispatched to the "friend zone," you should accept that a romantic relationship with this person simply wasn't meant to happen, and move on. A good way to do this is to occupy your time with healthy activities. Channel your negative energy into positive energy by indulging in your schoolwork, hobbies, after-school activities, or just talking with your friends. That's one of the reasons your friends are your friends—so that you can come to them in times of crisis. Also, it's a sure bet that your friends have also been the victims of rejection before and that each of them has been deposited in the friend zone at some point.

One reaction that would not be healthy is to turn around and ask someone else out right away, either to soothe your hurt feelings or to prove something to the person who rejected you. You should ask someone out only when you genuinely like her and want to create a special relationship, not when it's part of an agenda or an act of revenge or anger.

Furthermore, if the person you'd like to ask out is someone you've admired from afar (perhaps someone you've had a crush on for some time), it's a good idea to get to know the person socially before asking her or him out. Talk to the person at school, or spend time with her or him if you both happen to be at the same party. This way, in a relaxed, public setting, you can find out what the person's likes and dislikes are, if the two of you are into the same things, and if you feel comfortable around one another. Then, you can gauge whether there's a chance for you to move from being just friends to being something more.

It's important to stress that, when you're getting to know someone for the first time, and when you're in that early stage before you've asked her or him out, you should find out what the person likes and doesn't like (not just what likes and dislikes she or he shares with you). Make it a point to let the person know you're a good listener and that her or his thoughts, feelings, and opinions are important to you. Don't make the conversation all about yourself. If you sense that you've been talking about yourself too long, you can try to initiate a less self-involved conversational path by saying, "Enough about me. What was your day like today?" People like to be reminded that they are important and their feelings matter. If you make someone feel important and special even when talking casually, in a nonromantic context, chances are that the person will be more receptive when you actually ask her or him out.

If you're new to the dating scene, you should probably ask out someone you already know, or someone your friends know and like, rather than a complete stranger.

Dating Criteria

What makes someone good girlfriend/boyfriend material? First, you need to understand that there is no such thing as the perfect mate, despite what Hollywood romantic comedies, greeting cards, and love songs might say. There is, however, someone out there who shares your general worldview, who gets or understands you, and who accepts you for who you are. Someone who finds you attractive, someone who is happy to be around you and who makes you happy as well. In fact, there is probably a list of qualities you're looking for in the perfect girlfriend/boyfriend. You should write out just such a list, to crystallize your ideas of what you want in a significant other. You may not find all those qualities in one person, but at least you know what you're looking for and what you value in a person.

CHAPTER 6

Taking It to the Next Level—or Not

Let's assume that you've been dating someone for a few weeks or even a few months. At some point, there'll be a subject that one of you might want to broach. That subject is sex.

Are You Ready?

If you're not yet sexually active, you might want to weigh a few of the facts about sex before making any decisions to become active. Are you emotionally ready to have sex? If not, don't lie to yourself and pretend that you are. If the thought of having sex scares you or makes you nervous, don't be afraid to wait until it feels right. There's no shame in waiting. It actually shows great maturity and self-awareness. Your friends may tell you otherwise, and being a guy, it's possible that they've even teased you for wanting to wait. Just ignore them. This is your life and your body and your feelings and your relationship, not theirs.

Risks

There are some risks associated with sexual activity that you'll want to be aware of and watch out for. The most obvious one is the risk of contracting sexually transmitted diseases (STDs). Are you and your partner sexually active, but not using a condom? If so, there's a possibility that you might contract a sexually transmitted disease. The only surefire, completely safe way to assure that you won't expose yourself to an STD is by being abstinent, which means a total avoidance of sexual activity. It's also a good idea to know what some of the more severe STDs are. Two of them are HIV and herpes.

HIV, which stands for human immunodeficiency virus, is the virus that causes acquired immunodeficiency syndrome (AIDS). If you receive no treatment for HIV, the disease typically progresses to AIDS, and your body's immune system is weakened and has increasing trouble fighting off infections and disease. The end result is fatal. HIV can be transmitted in a few different ways, among them unprotected sexual contact (vaginal, oral, or anal) with someone who has HIV; through the breast milk of a nursing mother; from sharing needles or syringes that are contaminated with infected blood; or from a blood transfusion. This last one is a small risk because American hospitals and blood banks screen the blood supply for HIV antibodies. It's important to note that a man can get AIDS from female sexual partners as well as male partners.

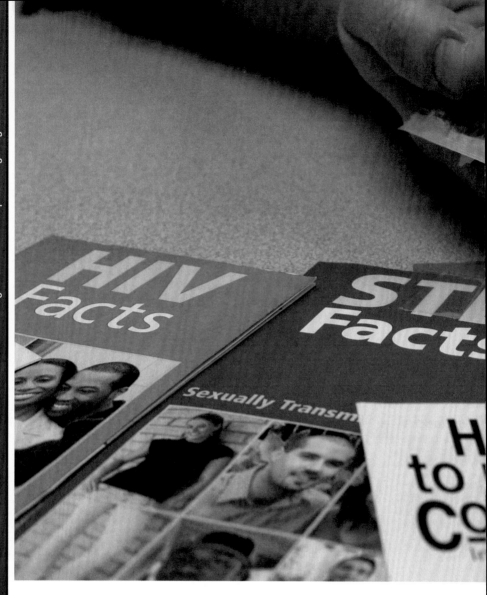

Herpes, like HIV, can be transmitted by unprotected sexual contact (vaginal, oral, or anal) with someone who has herpes. Herpes is caused by a virus called HSV, which stands for herpes simplex virus. HSV causes painful blisters, ulcers, or small red bumps to appear in the anal or genital areas. Many people who have HSV are unaware that they have been infected because the symptoms are so mild. However, it is unwise to risk sexual contact with someone

It's a good idea to educate yourself about the risks of sexual activity before making any decisions to have sex.

who might have herpes, especially since there is no cure. Other common STDs include syphilis, HPV (human papillomavirus), gonorrhea, viral hepatitis, chlamydia, pelvic inflammatory disease, and trichomoniasis. All have very serious implications for your health and the health of your partner. All can be prevented by abstinence. Condoms provide protection against only some of them (and not 100 percent protection).

One of the main risks of sexual activity is pregnancy. If you're not prepared to become a parent, you're probably not ready to have sex.

Another risk of sexual contact is pregnancy. If you and your girlfriend indulge in sexual activities, and neither of you is using either a condom or some other form of birth control, your girlfriend may become pregnant. Also, you can get a girl pregnant even if you're not having actual sexual intercourse (in which the penis

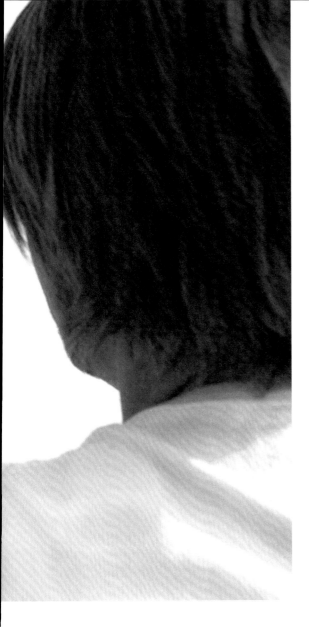

is inserted into the vagina). Any time your semen makes contact with a girl's genital area, even if the ejaculation occurs outside the vagina, there's the possibility that sperm will enter the vagina, fertilize an egg, and lead to pregnancy.

Even though your girlfriend is the one who might become pregnant, you'll be opening yourself up to the responsibilities of fatherhood, well before you might be emotionally or financially equipped to deal with them. Are you ready to spend the next couple of decades taking care of another human being? Before you decide to have sex, you should think very seriously about that possibility.

If your girlfriend is pregnant, the two of you can't go through this alone. You need to find an adult who is willing to help you and be supportive, whether that's one or both of your parents, one or both of your girlfriend's parents, or another adult that you trust. If you don't know anyone who fits that description, you should consult with a trusted doctor, therapist, or counselor. Seek referrals to a pregnancy or crisis counselor who can review and discuss all your options and give you some strategies for talking about this with your parents.

Reasonable Reasons?

Like people at any other stage of life, teenagers have sex for various reasons. Some of the most common reasons are:

- **Love, or a feeling of closeness to their partner.**
- **They want to know what it feels like:** This is quite common. As a teenager, especially if you haven't had sex before, the burning question—what's it like?—might be the subject of increasingly urgent curiosity. But this doesn't mean that you need to answer that burning question just yet, especially if you're not truly ready.
- **They want to lose their virginity:** Teenagers, and teenage boys in particular, often see their virginity as an albatross around their necks, a burden that must be lifted as soon as possible. However, lifting this "burden" is, in reality, not as urgent as it seems.
- **They want to satisfy a physical desire:** The desire to have sex is a nearly universal, primal urge. But one of the benefits that we human

beings have over our cousins in the animal kingdom is that we can overcome and control our primal urges for the good of ourselves and those around us. The decision to have sex should be a matter of the head and heart, not just the body and its urges.

Some of the above reasons are nobler than others, but on the whole, they're the result of simple, healthy, and typical urges, desires, and curiosity. On the other hand, some people have sex for the wrong reasons, such as:

- **Fear of loneliness:** You should never, ever have sex simply because you are feeling lonely or unloved.
- **Covering up (or ignoring) other issues:** Sex will not make the bad things in your life go away.
- **Trying to change someone:** If you think that having sex with someone will somehow make her or him a more attentive, sensitive, or thoughtful girlfriend/boyfriend, or that she or he will fall deeper in love with you after having sex, think again.
- **Being on the rebound:** It's never a good idea to have sex with someone merely to wipe away the memory of your previous sexual partner. This just leads to confusion, mixed emotions, and hurt feelings. For example, perhaps your partner was not aware that she/he was the recipient of "rebound sex." Don't you think your partner's feelings would be hurt by such news?

MYTHS and Facts

MYTH

It's just as easy for a long-distance relationship to thrive as it is for a relationship where both partners are in the same location.

Fact

Long-term relationships require an extraordinary amount of work, planning, communication, and patience to succeed.

MYTH

It's impossible for a long-distance relationship to last.

Fact

It isn't impossible for long-distance relationships to last; however, the physical distance between the two partners makes it more of a challenge.

MYTH

When I'm in a long-distance relationship, I should channel all of my time and energy into making the relationship work.

Fact

When you're separated from a girlfriend or boyfriend, you should be careful not to ignore your friends, family, hobbies, activities, schoolwork, or job. You need balance in your life, and you can't be completely focused on the relationship 100 percent of the time.

Cheating

It's normal, when dating one person, to wonder what it would be like to date someone else. However, there's a big difference between wondering what it would be like to be with someone else and not bothering to break up with your current partner before beginning to see someone new. If you and your partner have set up ground rules that say that neither of you is to date anyone else—if your relationship is exclusive—going outside of that relationship constitutes cheating.

People cheat for many reasons. Sometimes they cheat because they have trust issues or because they're insecure. Other times, they cheat because they just don't have any respect for the person they're with or because they lack basic maturity. In any case, cheating always hurts all the parties involved.

Perhaps you're considering cheating. If so, you should take a moment and think about what it is about your current

Seeing an ex-girlfriend with someone new is an incredibly painful experience. But you must find a way to move forward and look to the future. Don't live in the past!

relationship that's making you unhappy or dissatisfied or that's causing you to want to cheat. Think about how your cheating will affect your relationship with your significant other. Think about the shame and guilt you might feel after you've cheated. Last, but definitely not least, think about how awful you would feel if someone cheated on you. If you can imagine how miserable that would feel, you would never want to inflict that feeling on anyone else.

CHAPTER 7

Your Online Profile

Over the past couple of decades, the Internet has revolutionized the way we interact with media, the way we gather information, and the way we socialize. Thanks to social networking sites like Facebook and video-sharing sites like YouTube, teenagers can freely express themselves and share their thoughts, feelings, activities, and private lives with the larger public. This can be a creative and open-ended way to make new friends, keep in touch with old ones, announce and publicize events and milestones that you're proud of, and generally develop and maintain a distinctive Web presence. It's also a good way to make sure that your voice is heard and to speak out on subjects about which you're passionate. All of these things are positive. Yet social networking and online sharing can have their pitfalls and dangers, too.

Safety Risks

There are potential safety risks involved when establishing online friendships. Because of the fact that sites like

Beware of online predators! Someone who's claiming to be a sixteen-year-old girl online could actually be a forty-five-year-old man who is up to no good.

Friendster and Myspace aren't dating sites, they don't screen their users. However, they do serve as a destination for teens eager to meet new people. As such, they're a potential target for online predators.

When you create an online profile, it's easy to lie about who you are. For one thing, there's nothing stopping you from posting a picture of someone else and claiming that it's you. You can also lie about yourself when creating background information on a profile, and this false info can lend credibility to the lie. For example, if you post a photo of a football player on your profile, and you also post information saying that you're the star quarterback of your high school, but in real life you've never even thrown a football, much less played in a game, your online friends are none the wiser. Predators take advantage of this opportunity for deception. It's possible that someone claiming to be a sixteen-year-old girl could actually be a forty-five-year-old man who is up to no good and may wish to harm you or take advantage of you.

Safety Tips

There are some precautions you should take when you are chatting online with someone you haven't met in person. First, whenever communicating with someone online, always assume that the person you're dealing with is not whom he or she claims to be and act with an appropriate level of caution and defensiveness. The only exception to this would be if the person you're dealing with is someone you've actually met offline, in the "real" world. Also, never give out your personal information to anyone online. This includes your last name, address, phone numbers, bank account number, Social Security number, school's name and location, or the neighborhood you live in. Never send compromising pictures or videos of yourself, even to friends. All it takes is for one person to forward this to someone, and the images can go viral and remain accessible in cyberspace forever.

Cyberbullying

Bullies tend to concentrate on aspects of their targets' personal lives (i.e., their race, religion, sexual orientation,

YOUR CLASSIFIED INFORMATION

So, now that we've covered what information you cannot give out, what information can you give out if you're looking to form an online friendship? What little, nonidentifying information you do give out should be the truth. In other words, don't lie about your age because doing so could prove to be dangerous. Also, you can list your interests, goals, and personal accomplishments, and you can talk about your personality.

weight, and height). These are the very characteristics people are encouraged to post within their online profiles on social networking sites. This gives the bully easy access to material which he or she can then use to bully you in an even more public forum than the hallway of your school.

In addition, the Internet encourages creative and often very personal self-expression. This can be a good thing, and it's yielded any number of positive outcomes, from funny comedy videos being posted on YouTube to some of the smarter and more insightful blogs out there. However, the downside is that, thanks to the Internet, a bully also has a forum for self-expression. The bully's self-expression takes the form of cruel rants and taunts, often in direct, mocking response to what you have posted. The purpose of cyberbullying is to intentionally embarrass, harass, intimidate, or make threats online to someone else.

What constitutes cyberbullying? According to the Web site schoolbullyingcouncil.com, cyberbullying is when "an electronic device is used to attack or defame the character of a real person." Cyberbullying occurs via e-mail, text messaging, blog posts or comments, and Web sites. This can be done by posting embarrassing and untrue information on an online forum, where the victim and the victim's friends and family—not to mention complete strangers—can see this information publicly. Other examples of cyberbullying include sending threatening or overtly sexual e-mails to someone who doesn't want any contact with the sender.

Recently, legislation has been passed to combat cyberbullying, and awareness campaigns have been organized for the same purpose. Cyberbullying has become a hot-button topic because, before the Internet (and specifically the rise of social networking sites over the past decade), no one had access to this ultra-public form of taunting and intimidation. In the past, if a bully wanted to pick on someone, it was basically a one-on-one situation, with perhaps a few of the victim's fellow students looking on. Now, however, a bully can post horrible and often untrue things about someone he or she doesn't like on a social networking site. Literally millions of people can see it, post comments on it, and publicly shame someone, adding fuel to the bully's fire. This sort of public humiliation is very psychologically damaging, and no one—particularly no young person—deserves it.

The Online Bandwagon

Unlike traditional, in-person bullies, cyberbullies can hide behind the protective wall of cyberspace, thereby remaining anonymous—and incredibly cowardly. By using e-mail accounts, pseudonyms (fake names) in chat rooms, instant messaging, text messaging, and the comments section of blogs, they can easily hide their true identities while saying

Imagine how awful it would feel to read something embarrassing, humiliating, hurtful, or untrue about yourself on the Internet. This is why you should never instigate or join in cyberbullying. It is a grave violation of someone's privacy and personhood.

vicious, hateful, and untrue things about a person. This frees cyberbullies from the fear of getting caught. If you don't know who the culprit is, how will he or she be punished? If there's no fear of punishment and exposure, what will hold the bully back from unleashing his or her cowardice and hatefulness?

This sense of anonymity also encourages the sort of "bandwagon" mentality of cyberbullying. If a cyberbully posts something nasty about his or her victim, then many people might post equally nasty responses to the initial post. They somehow feel permitted and emboldened to do so now that the first negative comment has been made. Soon there is a domino effect, which works in favor of the cyberbully. Some might not even know the victim, but they find the cyberbully's antics so humorous that they comment on it, adding to the victim's misery.

This is also a phenomenon that is particular to the Internet: people will often say something really cruel online that they wouldn't say to your face. That's because when you're saying something hurtful about someone online, you don't have to look the person in the eye. There's a distance there. Your target seems less like a real person and more like just a number, one of many, out there in cyberspace. But that target is not a number. He or she is a person with feelings.

As a young man in today's world, you may be under pressure from your friends to join in cyberbullying, by making fun of someone in an online forum. Perhaps you don't even think of it as bullying. You just consider it good-natured joking around or the price people pay for expressing themselves freely online. Think again. The person you're making fun of doesn't like it, and you wouldn't want it done to you. Imagine if all your classmates, your teachers, your friends, and your family members were reading horrible, embarrassing, humiliating things written about you (or viewed compromising photos or videos of you). And it was all being forwarded to thousands of people, who in turn forwarded it to thousands more.

Victims of cyberbullying have undergone treatment for stress, anxiety, and depression. In some cases, they've even committed suicide. This is no laughing matter. If your friends want you to join in this sort of "joking around," just say no. And consider making new friends.

CHAPTER 8

ALL GOOD THINGS

As the saying goes, all good things must come to an end. Yet they are often replaced by other, sometimes even better, things. Not all relationships are destined to last forever. As a teenage boy, you may be in the midst of your first romantic relationship. Perhaps this is the person you'll spend the rest of your life with, but the odds are against that. The typical adolescent male falls in and out of love several times during this period of his life, and that's completely normal. Perhaps you were once in love with your significant other, but it seems that things have … changed lately.

"It's Not You, It's Me"

Usually, problems arise in a romantic relationship because one person is hiding things from, or not being honest with, the other person. When the couple isn't openly and honestly communicating, a lack of trust develops, and this leads to dishonesty, wariness, and resentment. One of the ways in which dishonesty manifests itself is in one partner cheating on the other. However, sometimes one partner blames his or her problems on the other partner, or one partner insults the other partner and hurts his or her self-esteem. On the other hand, a couple that communicates honestly with each other about their individual problems, issues, and insecurities is bound to have a healthier relationship than one in which one or both partners are keeping things inside.

This isn't a foolproof formula for romantic happiness, however. It's possible that even a couple that has tried talking about their problems will still hit a rough patch. Maybe that couple is going around in circles, arguing about the same things over and over again. Or, maybe the two people in the relationship aren't the same two people they were when that relationship began. This is certainly probable during your teen years, when your wants, needs, and interests change dramatically in the space of a short period of time.

If you've considering breaking up with your significant other, you should know that all breakups are difficult. There's no way to let someone down easy. Hurt feelings and anger are pretty much inevitable. However, while you can't make the breakup easy, you can make the breakup easier. You can do this by being open, honest, and sensitive during the breakup. How can you do that?

For one thing, you should be honest about why you're breaking up with your girlfriend or boyfriend. Don't make up a flimsy excuse. If you've met someone else, your soon-to-be-ex deserves to know. On the other hand, if you feel that you've grown apart from your significant other, and you feel you don't have anything in common anymore, come clean about that as well. Also, don't send someone else to break the

Being up front with your partner about the reasons for your unhappiness and breaking up in person are things that you owe her or him.

news, and don't break up over the phone or via text or e-mail. Being up front with your partner and breaking up in person is something that you owe her or him, and doing this through a third party will cause much anger and resentment.

Also, don't try to force your significant other to break up with you first, by cheating on or abusing her or him. Abusing someone, either physically, verbally, or emotionally, is never the solution. It will leave psychological scars for your partner that may take a long time to heal. Furthermore, it's the act of a coward. Do you want to be that kind of person? Honor the love you once felt for that person, and in some ways still do, by treating her or him in as kind, compassionate, and caring a manner as possible.

♂ DOWN IN THE DUMPS

But what if you're not the one doing the breaking up? What if you're the one who's been dumped? This is never easy, and often it's extremely painful emotionally. You may walk around in a daze for some time, feeling not quite like yourself. It's important during this difficult time to reach out to those close to you.

Everyone has a support system to call upon in times of crisis, whether it's your circle of friends, a sibling, a parent, or a favorite aunt or uncle. These are the people who understand what you're going through—after all, they've most likely been through it themselves—and you can feel comfortable telling them about how upset you are. Remember, it is not "unmanly" to talk about your problems and your emotions, even to other guys. In fact, if your friends are really your friends, they'll understand where you're coming from and help you feel better about it. And your willingness to express your feelings of hurt and sadness show real courage.

The postbreakup period is a good time to concentrate on yourself and to work on other aspects of your life. Perhaps there are activities or hobbies that you'd neglected during the relationship—now you can have fun working on them! It's also a good idea to do things that make you feel good about yourself, such as exercising and eating right. Doing both will help you feel more self-confident and empowered, and they'll stop you from dwelling on the pain of the breakup.

What Does It All Mean?

One cliché you've probably heard as a teenage boy is that these are the best years of your life. You have youth, energy, physical health, and wide-open horizons. But wouldn't it be sad if everything went downhill for you after you reached the age of twenty? For this reason, it's a good idea not to think of your adolescence as the best years of your life, but rather as a really wonderful, positive period of growth that leads to an equally wonderful, positive adulthood.

The amazing thing about your teenage years, and the reason most people mistakenly refer to this period as the best years of your life, is because you don't have to pay for things like bills, groceries, room and board, or almost anything else. It's the last time in your life when you can say that. You'll also make friends during high school and college that you may keep in contact with for the rest of your life. In terms of your love life, you'll go through your first real adult relationships. That, in and of itself, is exciting. However, the flip side is that your teen years are also a time in your life when there's much that seems frightening, new, scary, and awkward. You don't always know how to act or what paths to take, and the guideposts are not always clear. You no longer have parents always telling you what to do and how to do it. You're making some of your own decisions independently, and that is both exhilarating and terrifying.

Harry Potter actor Daniel Radcliffe visits the Trevor Project, which helps to prevent suicides among LGBT youth.

But rest assured that it does get better. There is life beyond adolescence. Consider the fact that many of the most successful businesspeople, artists, performers, and filmmakers weren't exactly considered the cool kids at their high school. On the other hand, if you're one of the more athletic students at your school, the discipline and self-confidence you learned performing at your best is something you'll be able to apply to many of your goals as an adult. The most important lesson you'll learn from your teen years, however, is that relationships matter. Your bond with your friends, family members, and significant others will deepen during this period. These are people who care as deeply about you as you do about them, and they'll be there for you no matter what.

adolescence The period between the beginning of puberty and adulthood.

articulate To express oneself verbally in a clear and coherent manner.

bullying The act of intimidating someone, to make the person do something he or she wouldn't ordinarily do. Bullying can include actions that are physical and/or verbal, such as violent behavior, exclusion, threats, gossip, and body language.

clique A small, exclusive group of people, especially one held together by common views or interests.

cyberspace A worldwide system of computer networks, in which online communication takes place. The term "cyberspace" is frequently used to describe the Internet.

diversity The state or quality of being different. In the modern sense, the term "diversity" is often used to discuss the understanding and acceptance of all people, regardless of ethnicity, culture, gender, or sexual orientation.

emotional vocabulary The words used to communicate one's feelings, both to the outside world and oneself.

frenemy Someone who pretends to be your friend, but who is really your enemy. "Frenemy" can also refer to a friend with whom you have a combative relationship or a colleague who is also your rival.

machismo A strong sense of masculinity or masculine pride and a desire to show it off or prove it publicly.

ostracize To exclude from a group, especially by popular consent.

paradigm shift A change in a basic way of thinking from an accepted point of view to a new one. Paradigm shifts are often brought on when scientific discoveries or societal revolutions bring on radical changes in the worldview of the culture at large.

peer pressure Social pressure brought on by one's peer group to adopt a certain type of attitude, behavior, or dress in order to be accepted.

sexual orientation The direction of one's sexual attraction toward members of the same, opposite, or both sexes.

stereotype A simple or commonly held belief about specific social groups or types of people. Also, to treat or classify someone according to a preconceived notion that one might have about the group to which that person belongs.

stress A mental state, such as anxiety, or a physical state, such as injury, that prevents the mind or body from functioning normally.

Big Brothers Big Sisters of America
National Office
230 North 13th Street
Philadelphia, PA 19107
(215) 567-7000
Web site: http://www.bbbs.org
Big Brothers Big Sisters of America is a mentoring organization whose volunteers
provide advice and support to youth.

Boys & Girls Club
National Headquarters
1275 Peachtree Street NE
Atlanta, GA 30309-3506
(404) 487-5700
Web site: http://www.bgca.org
The Boys & Girls Club provides a safe venue for children to grow and learn, as well as
a way to foster ongoing relationships with caring adult professionals. The
organization offers programs and experiences designed to build character and
enhance children's lives.

Health Canada
Address Locator 0900C2
Ottawa, ON K1A 0K9
Canada
(613) 957-2991
Web site: http://www.hc-sc.gc.ca

Health Canada is the federal department responsible for helping the people of Canada maintain and improve their health. It offers many resources on teen issues like bullying, online safety, teen pregnancy, diet and exercise, alcohol and drug abuse, body image, depression, family issues, risky behaviors, and sexuality and relationships.

Media Awareness Network (MNet)
950 Gladstone Avenue, Suite 120
Ottawa, ON K1Y 3E6
Canada
(613) 224-7721
(800) 896-3342 (in Canada)
Web site: http://www.media-awareness.ca

MNet is a Canadian nonprofit organization that has been pioneering the development of media literacy and digital literacy programs since its incorporation in 1996. It is home to one of the world's most comprehensive collections of media literacy and digital literacy resources. MNet focuses its efforts on developing the information and tools necessary to help young people understand how the media work, how the media may affect their lifestyle choices, and the extent to which they, as consumers and citizens, are being well informed.

National Youth Leadership Council (NYLC)
1667 Snelling Avenue North
St. Paul, MN 55108
(651) 631-3672
Web site: http://www.nylc.org

The NYLC is devoted to helping young people become leaders in their communities via community involvement.

Parents, Families, and Friends of Lesbians and Gays (PFLAG)
1276 M Street NW, Suite 400
Washington, DC 20036
(202) 467-8180
Web site: http://www.pflag.org
Via support, education, and advocacy, PFLAG promotes the well-being and health of gay, lesbian, bisexual, and transgendered people, as well as their family and friends.

Students Against Destructive Decisions (SADD)
P.O. Box 800
Marlboro, MA 01752
(877) SADD-INC (723-3462)
Web site: http://www.saddonline.com
SADD is a student-based organization originally founded to combat underage drinking and drunk driving. Since then, it has expanded its mission to address issues such as drug abuse, violence, STDs, and suicide.

The Trevor Project
Administrative Offices
8704 Santa Monica Boulevard, Suite 200
West Hollywood, CA 90069
(310) 271-8845

Web site: http://www.thetrevorproject.org
An organization that provides life-affirming support for GLBT teens.

YMCA
5 West 63rd Street, 2nd Floor
New York, NY 10023
(212) 727-8800
Toll Free: (888) 477-9622
Web site: http://www.ymca.net
The YMCA offers young people a place to come after school for safe, productive activities that support academic achievement, encourage self-confidence, and develop healthy lifestyles.

Web Sites

Due to the changing nature of Internet links, Rosen Publishing has developed an online list of Web sites related to the subject of this book. This site is updated regularly. Please use this link to access the list:

http://www.rosenlinks.com/ymg/dare

Beckman, Wendy Hart. *Dating, Relationships, and Sexuality: What Teens Should Know.* Berkeley Heights, NJ: Enslow Publishers, 2006.

Boyett, Jason. *A Guy's Guide to Life: How to Become a Man in 224 Pages or Less.* Nashville, TN: Thomas Nelson, 2010.

Braner, Andy. *An Exposé on Teen Sex and Dating: What's Really Going On and How to Talk About It.* Colorado Springs, CO: NavPress, 2011.

Canfield, Jack, and Mark Victor Hansen. *Chicken Soup for the Soul: Teens Talk Relationships: Stories About Family, Friends, and Love.* Cos Cob, CT: Chicken Soup for the Soul Publishing, 2008.

Covey, Sean. *The 6 Most Important Decisions You'll Ever Make: A Guide for Teens.* New York, NY: Fireside, 2006.

Eastham, Chad. *The Truth About Dating, Love, and Just Being Friends.* Nashville, TN: Thomas Nelson, 2011.

Eastham, Chad, Bill Farrel, and Pam Farrel. *Guys Are Waffles, Girls Are Spaghetti.* Nashville, TN: Thomas Nelson, 2009.

Feldhahn, Jeff, Eric Rice, and Shaunti Feldhahn. *For Young Men Only: A Guy's Guide to the Alien Gender.* Colorado Springs, CO: Multnomah Books, 2008.

Heiden, Pete. *I Luv U 2: Understanding Relationships and Dating* (Essential Health: A Guy's Guide). Edina, MN: ABDO Publishing, 2010.

Levy, Barrie. *In Love and in Danger: A Teen's Guide to Breaking Free of Abusive Relationships*. New York, NY: Seal Press, 2006.

Mayo, Jeanne. *Uncensored—Dating, Friendship, and Sex: You Think You Know, But You Have No Idea*. Tulsa, OK: Harrison House, 2007.

Payment, Simone. *Friendship, Dating, and Relationships* (Teens: Being Gay, Lesbian, Bisexual, or Transgender). New York, NY: Rosen Publishing, 2010.

Abernathy, Michael. "Male Bashing on TV." Popmatters. com, January 9, 2003. Retrieved February 2011 (http://www.popmatters.com/tv/features/030109-male-bashing.shtml).

Armstrong, Jennifer. "Gay Teens on TV." *Entertainment Weekly*, January 28, 2011.

Bass, Ellen, and Kate Kaufman. *Free Your Mind: The Book for Gay, Lesbian, and Bisexual Youth—And Their Allies*. New York, NY: Harper Perennial, 1996.

Chafkin, Max. "How to Kill a Great Idea!" Inc., June 1, 2007. Retrieved February 2011 (http://www.inc. com/magazine/20070601/features-how-to-kill-a-great-idea.html).

Clark-Flory, Tracy. "Teenage Boys Not So Sex Crazed?" Salon.com, February 25, 2008. Retrieved January 2011 (http://www.salon.com/life/broadsheet/ 2008/02/25/boys).

Cruz, Gilbert. "The Internet: Safe for Kids?" *Time*, January 15, 2009. Retrieved January 2011 (http://www.time. com/time/nation/article/0,8599,1871664,00.html).

Cullen, Kevin. "The Untouchable Mean Girls." *Boston Globe*, January 24, 2010. Retrieved January 2011 (http://www.boston.com/community/moms/articles/ 2010/01/24/the_untouchable_mean_girls).

Cullen, Murray C., and Wright, Joan. *Cage Your Rage for Teens: A Guide to Anger*. Lanham, MD: American Correctional Association, 1996.

Dentemaro, Christine, and Rachel Kranz. *Straight Talk About Anger*. New York, NY: Facts On File, 1995.

Eyre, Linda, and Richard Eyre. *Teaching Your Children Responsibility*. Salt Lake City, UT: Shadow Mountain, 1984.

Fox, Annie M., ed. *The Teen Survival Guide to Dating & Relating: Real-World Advice on Guys, Girls, Growing Up, and Getting Along*. Minneapolis, MN: Free Spirit Publishing, 2005.

Gaines, Donna. *Teenage Wasteland: Suburbia's Dead End Kids*. New York, NY: Pantheon Books, 1991.

Goleman, Daniel. *Emotional Intelligence: Why It Can Matter More Than IQ*. New York, NY: Bantam Books. 1995.

Grossman, Lev. "The Secret Love Lives of Teenage Boys." *Time*, August 27. 2006. Retrieved December 2010 (http://www.time.com/time/magazine/article/ 0,9171,1376235,00.html).

Hamburger, Lew. *Winning! How Teens (and Other Humans) Can Beat Anger and Depression*. New York, NY: Vantage Press, 1997.

Hardcastle, Mike. "Meeting People Online: The Do's and Don'ts of Online Relationships for Teens." About.com. Retrieved February 2011 (http://teenadvice.about. com/od/streetsmarts/a/onlinefriends.htm).

Hoffman, Todd. "Popular Culture's War on Men." *McGill Reporter*, November 8, 2001. Retrieved February 2011 (http://www.mcgill.ca/reporter/34/05/misandry).

Howe, Neil, and William Strauss. *Millennials Rising: The Next Great Generation.* New York, NY: Vintage Books, 2000.

Kindlon, Dan, and Michael Thompson. *Raising Cain: Protecting the Emotional Life of Boys.* New York, NY: Ballantine Books, 2000.

Klinger, Ron. "What Can Be Done About Absentee Fathers?" *USA Today* (Society for the Advancement of Education), July 1998. Retrieved February 2011 (http://findarticles.com/p/articles/mi_m1272/is_n2638_v127/ai_20954306).

Muharrar, Aisha. *More Than a Label: Why What You Wear or Who You're with Doesn't Define Who You Are.* Minneapolis, MN: Free Spirit Publishing, 2002.

Parker-Pope, Tara. "Inside the Mind of the Boy Dating Your Daughter." *New York Times,* February 15, 2008. Retrieved December 2010 (http://well.blogs.nytimes.com/2008/02/15/inside-the-mind-of-the-boy-dating-your-daughter).

Parker-Pope, Tara. "Peeking Inside the Mind of the Boy Dating Your Daughter. *New York Times,* February 24, 2008. Retrieved December 2010 (http://www.nytimes.com/2008/02/24/weekinreview/24parker.html).

Perez-Pena, Richard. "Christie Signs Tougher Law on Bullying in Schools." *New York Times,* January 6, 2011. Retrieved January 2011 (http://www.nytimes.com/2011/01/07/nyregion/07bully.html).

Riera, Michael. *Staying Connected to Your Teenager: How to Keep Them Talking to You and How to Hear What They're Really Saying.* Cambridge, MA: DaCapo Press, 2003.

Taddonio, Elizabeth. "Online Dating Safety Lessons for Teens." eHow, August 11, 2010. Retrieved February 2011 (http://www.ehow.com/print/list_6832639_online-dating-safety-lessons-teens.html).

Tatum, Beverly Daniel. *"Why Are All the Black Kids Sitting Together in the Cafeteria?" and Other Conversation Starters About Race.* New York, NY: Basic Books, 1999.

Voo, Jocelyn. "Do You Have a 'Frenemy'?" CNN.com, August 27, 2007. Retrieved January 2011 (http://www.cnn.com/2007/LIVING/personal/08/24/frenemies/index.html).

About the Author

Arie Kaplan has written numerous books on pop culture, cultural studies, history, and youth culture. He's also written for such teen-oriented magazines as *Teen Beat*, *Bop*, and *Tiger Beat*. In addition, he's the author of *From Krakow to Krypton: Jews and Comic Books* (Jewish Publication Society), which was named a Booklist Editors' Choice: Books for Youth Winner for 2009. *From Krakow to Krypton* was also a 2008 finalist for the National Jewish Book Award, a 2009 Sophie Brody Honor Book (awarded by the American Library Association), and a 2009 National "Best Books 2009" Awards Finalist (awarded by USA Book News). Kaplan's other books for Rosen Publishing include *Blogs: Finding Your Voice, Finding Your Audience*. As a guest speaker, Kaplan travels all over the world and lectures on various subjects, including the history of comic books, film, comedy, and other aspects of pop culture. He has also written for MTV, Cartoon Network, and PBS Kids.

Photo Credits

Cover (front and back), pp. 9, 19, 30, 40, 50, 64, 76, 83 © www.istockphoto.com/Catherine Lane; pp. 6–7 Lifesize/Thinkstock.com; pp. 10–11 Polka Dot/Thinkstock.com; pp. 14–15 © North County Times/ZUMApress.com; p. 17 www.istockphotock.com/Helder Almeida; p. 20 Image Source/Getty Images; pp. 22–23, 58–59, 81 Shutterstock.com; p. 26 © www.istockphoto.com/Catherine Yeulet; pp. 28, 52–53 Stockbyte/Thinkstock.com; pp. 32–33 © www.istockphoto.com/digitalskillet; p. 35 © www.istockphoto.com/Joseph Abbott; pp. 38–39 © Focus Features/Courtesy Everett Collection; pp. 42–43 Allan Shoemake/Photodisc/Getty Images; pp. 46–47 Comstock/Thinkstock.com; pp. 48, 77 iStockphoto/Thinkstock.com; pp. 54–55, 62 Photodisc/Thinkstock.com; pp. 66–67 William Wan/The Washington Post/Getty Images; pp. 68–69 © Westend61/SuperStock; pp. 74–75 © www.istockphoto.com/Josef Philipp; p. 85 AbleStock.com/Thinkstock.com; p. 88 Andrew H. Walker/Getty Images.

Designer: Les Kanturek; Photo Researcher: Amy Feinberg